For M.

Copyright © 1987 by Richard Stine

Published in 1995 by Welcome Enterprises, Inc.,
575 Broadway, New York, NY 10012
Distributed by Stewart, Tabori & Chang, Inc.,
575 Broadway, New York, NY 10012
Distributed in Canada by General Publishing Company Limited,
30 Lesmill Road, Don Mills, Ontario, M3B 2T6, Canada
Distributed in the U.K. by Hi Marketing,
38 Carver Road, London SE24 9LT, England
Distributed in Europe by Onslow Books Limited,
Tyler's Court, 111A Wardour Street, London W1V 3TD, England
Distributed in Australia and New Zealand by Peribo Pty Limited,
58 Beaumont Road, Mount Kuring-gai NSW, 2080, Australia

Originally published in 1987 by Simon & Schuster.

Printed and bound in Singapore by Tien Wah Press

10 9 8 7 6 5 4 3 2 1

Library of Congress Catalog Card Number: 95-090454

ISBN: 0-941807-01-0

OFF To SEA

A Romance

By Richard Stine

WELCOME ENTERPRISES, INC.

NEW YORK

There was a man.

There was a woman.

They met

and were drawn together in a
sea of mysterious attraction.

And for awhile they both said YES, YES

and they both said NO, NO

and all was harmonious...

until the day when one said NO
and one said YES

and one said YES and one said NO.

Then came the anger

and then the fighting

and then the barriers

and then the isolation,

and each wondered why. But there was no answer, so each went away...

One went this way,

and one went that way,

and each went off to see.

And this is what happened...

One walked in the stars

and one walked on the earth.

And one went to the edge of space

and one went to the end of time.

And one went to hell

and one went to heaven.

And one had pleasure

and one had pain.

And one saw death

and one saw birth.

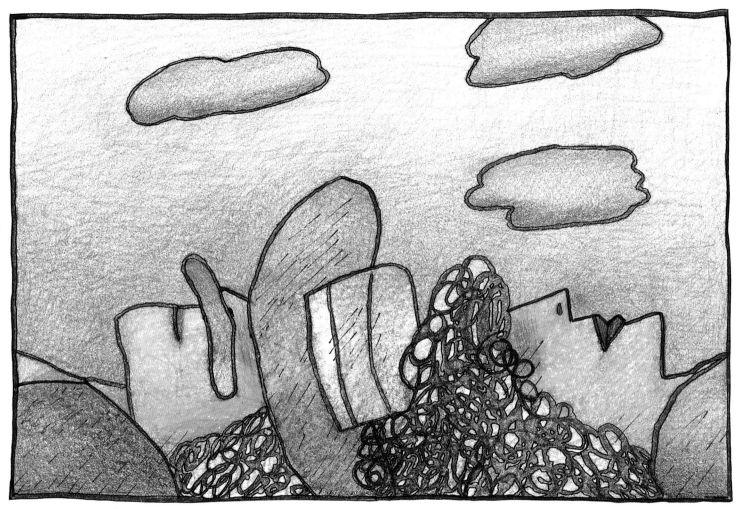

And they returned from it all, met again and
realized they had both gone far and experienced
much. And for that they bowed respectfully
to each other and lay down to rest.
And in their sleep they dreamed...

They dreamed of a Great Sea

and from the sea came a heart.

And the heart grew larger and larger

and larger . . .

Until it grew so large it could not be contained and it burst into pieces.

And every piece
became something,
And all the pieces
became everything...

The birds

and the clouds and the trees

and the bugs

and the people

and the cars

and the rocks

and everything else.

And for awhile all
were happy and content
to be, to do, to want
and to get...

And the fish swam

and the birds flew

and the trees grew.

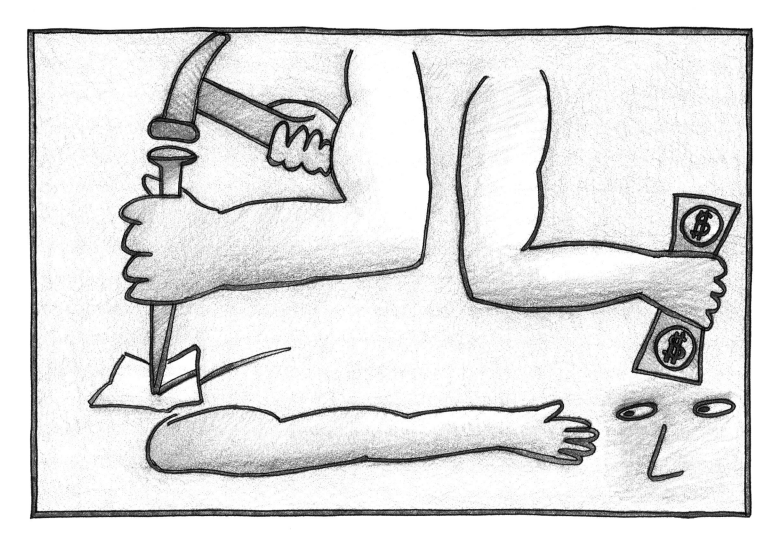

And people were, did, wanted and got.

But in time, being
and doing and want-
ing and getting were not
enough. At last, because
of all the unhappiness,
a decision was

made to unite again,
each in the heart as
part of the heart. And
that, by great effort,
is what they did.
And the dream ended.

The man and woman awakened and knew they had dreamed the same dream, and they smiled.

Time passed and the man entered himself and found many treasures,

and the woman entered herself
and found many riches.

And by those discoveries, each was strengthened.

And with that strength, the man
entered the woman

and the woman entered the man.

And together as one

they saw pleasure and pain, time and space, heaven and hell, birth and death, and everything else unite in their essence.

And they were cleansed and deepened beyond themselves, and there they found Love.

And by that path they entered the heart,

whose home is in the Great Sea,

whose home

is in the dream...

And
the
Dream
is
Real.